Bod
and the Cake

Michael and Joanne Cole

EGMONT

EGMONT

We bring stories to life

Original paperback edition first published in Great Britain 1977 by Methuen & Co. Ltd.
This edition first published in Great Britain 2016 by Egmont UK Limited,
The Yellow Building, 1 Nicholas Road, London W11 4AN
www.egmont.co.uk

ISBN 978 1 4052 8056 3

A CIP catalogue record for this title is available from the British Library.

MIX
Paper from
responsible sources
FSC® C018306

Here comes Aunt Flo. It's her baking day
and she's in a baking mood.
"A real cake baking mood," she says.

She gets her big mixing bowl and puts
in everything she needs to make a rich
fruit cake. She stirs away.
"What stirring times we live in," she says.

"I'm going to need help eating this cake."
She phones up Bod to ask him to tea,
and also asks him to invite Frank, Barleymow
and P.C. Copper for her, as she's so busy.

"Oh, and would you phone me just before you come to remind me to take the cake out of the oven?" says Aunt Flo. "You know how forgetful I've grown."

"I won't forget," says Bod. "I'll just do another piece of my jigsaw before I ring. Now, where can it go? Here . . . no . . . there . . . no . . . where?"

Then he rings Farmer Barleymow, who takes
some time to answer the phone as he's busy
feeding his pigs.
Bod gives him Aunt Flo's message.

"How could I miss one of Flo's cakes?"
says Barleymow.
"Would you mind phoning the others and
asking them too?" says Bod. "I'm a bit busy."

"I'll just put the cows in," says Barleymow.

"Come on, Gertrude, move yourself."
Gertrude is the slowest cow.

Then he phones Frank the Postman.
"Aunt Flo is making a cake," says Barleymow.
"Can you come?"
"Nothing could stop me," says Frank.

"Would you mind phoning P.C. Copper and asking him too?" says Barleymow. "I must get the mud off my boots and have a good wash."

"I'll just finish papering this wall," says Frank.
"It won't take a jiffy."

But it takes several jiffies. And not all of the
paper goes on the wall.

Some of it gets stuck to Frank. He dials the
police with sticky fingers, and asks to speak
to P.C. Copper.
"Hello," says P.C. Copper.

Frank gives him the message.
"Haven't had one of Flo's cakes for years,"
says P.C. Copper. "The last one was a sponge
I'll never forget."

"I'll just sort out this traffic jam first.

I don't want jam for tea – especially traffic
jam. I want Flo's cake."

He moves the traffic on,
and signals that it's safe to cross.

"What do you think she's made this time?" says
P.C. Copper. "Fruit, sponge or chocolate cake?"

Aunt Flo is busy getting ready for the tea party. She sweeps and dusts to make everything spic and span.

She gets out her best tea service and lays
the table. She picks some tulips from the
garden to put in a vase.

There's a knock at the door. Bod and his friends are there. When he sees Aunt Flo, Bod remembers that he didn't remind her to take the cake out of the oven.

"I'm terribly sorry," says Bod. "I don't know what to say. It must be burned to a cinder."
"It isn't," says Aunt Flo. "I've just remembered – I forgot to put it in."

"Never mind," says Aunt Flo. "Now you're
all here, let's have tea just the same. Will you
help me make some sandwiches, Bod?"
"Certainly," says Bod.

Frank, Barleymow and P.C. Copper
are very disappointed there's no cake.
But they don't show it. "What lovely
sandwiches," they say.

"I'll put the cake in the oven now," says Aunt Flo.
"And then you can all come and have tea again
with me tomorrow.

The cake will be just right then."

After tea, they all help clear away. Bod does the washing up, and the others do the drying up.

Barleymow takes care of the saucers and plates,
Frank the cups, and P.C. Copper the larger items.

They all say goodbye to Aunt Flo.
"By the way," says Bod, "how will
you remind yourself about the cake?"
"I'll tie a knot in my handkerchief," says Aunt Flo,
"and hope I remember what it means. Goodbye."